A Woman of Noble Character

By

TONIA L. RILEY

Scriptures are taken from the KING JAMES VERSION (KJV): KING JAMES VERSION, public domain.

To request permissions, contact the publisher: thewritelegacypublishing@gmail.com

ISBN: 978-1-955418-02-7

Published by The Write Legacy, LLC
Powder Springs, Georgia
www.thewritelegacy.com
Printed in the U.S.A.

DEDICATION

To my husband, George, thank you for walking this
journey with me. This book *IS* because you pushed me,
you wouldn't let me give up. And to our children, you
guys are my inspiration, my legacy.

A WOMAN OF NOBLE CHARACTER

Proverbs 31:10-31 KJV

10 Who can find a virtuous woman? for her price is far above rubies.

11 The heart of her husband doth safely trust in her, so that he shall have no need of spoil.

12 She will do him good and not evil all the days of her life.

13 She seeketh wool, and flax, and worketh willingly with her hands.

14 She is like the merchants' ships; she bringeth her food from afar.

15 She riseth also while it is yet night, and giveth meat to her household, and a portion to her maidens.

16 She considereth a field, and buyeth it: with the fruit of her hands she planteth a vineyard.

17 She girdeth her loins with strength, and strengtheneth her arms.

18 She perceiveth that her merchandise is good: her candle goeth not out by night.

1

19 She layeth her hands to the spindle, and her hands hold the distaff.

20 She stretcheth out her hand to the poor; yea, she reacheth forth her hands to the needy.

21 She is not afraid of the snow for her household: for all her household are clothed with scarlet.

22 She maketh herself coverings of tapestry; her clothing is silk and purple.

23 Her husband is known in the gates, when he sitteth among the elders of the land.

24 She maketh fine linen, and selleth it; and delivereth girdles unto the merchant.

25 Strength and honour are her clothing; and she shall rejoice in time to come.

26 She openeth her mouth with wisdom; and in her tongue is the law of kindness.

27 She looketh well to the ways of her household, and eateth not the bread of idleness.

28 Her children arise up, and call her blessed; her husband also, and he praiseth her.

29 Many daughters have done virtuously, but thou excellest them all.

30 Favour is deceitful, and beauty is vain: but a woman that feareth the Lord, she shall be praised. 31 Give her of the fruit of her hands; and let her own works praise her in the gates.

DADDY'S LITTLE PRINCESS

My name is Princess Tonia.
I know some of you may have laughed when you read that,
but my Daddy told me that I was his little princess.
You see, as a baby Christian I used to dance & twirl my
dress around & around before him dancing to impress
him as a young girl would her natural father.
And then he would pick me up and sit me on his lap and I
would sip spiritual milk but now that I'm old, I still dance
for him but it's to give him praise and instead of sitting on
his lap I sit at the table with him, feasting on the Word of
Life, eating wisdom & drinking knowledge, I've indulged
in joy & peace,
I am so stuffed with love & kindness. Seeing that I am so
full my Daddy walks me away from the table,
takes me to the hall closet and clothes me with strength. He
gently touches my face with both hands, looks me in the
eyes and tells me, "Now! Now my child,
go! Go out into all the world and do what I
have equipped you to do.
Go and bring your brothers and sisters home.
They're blind and can't see their way home."

"And I will be a father to you, and you will be my sons and daughters" says the Lord Almighty." **2 Corinthians 6:18 (NIV)**

"For ye have not received the spirit of bondage again to fear; but ye have received the spirit of adoption, whereby we cry, Abba, Father. The Spirit itself beareth witness with our spirit, that we are the children of God."
Romans 8:15-16 (KJV)

"And the Lord said unto the servant, go out into the highways and hedges, and compel them to come in, that my house may be filled."
Luke 14:23 (KJV)

"The fruit of the righteous is a tree of life; and he that winneth souls is wise."
Proverbs 11: 30 (KJV)

For some of us, seeing ourselves as *daddy's little princess* is difficult. We sometimes compare our relationship with God to the one of our natural fathers and how we see our natural father. The truth is it matters how we see God. Identity comes at the revelation of the Father. The relationship with Him is what causes you to find your identity. Dethrone your limitation, the strongholds, for the Father has equipped you to be who God says you are. Detach yourself from your failures, mistakes, your past and upbringing. Then know that you are loved by God. 1 John 3:1(NIV), "See what great love the father has lavished on us, that we should be called children of God! And that is what we are! "Know it and accept it in your heart. Embrace Daddy's love for you, ABBA has adopted you as his own. You are daddy's Princess. Be secure in his love, and then go out and share his love with others to win the souls of the lost to Christ. Let the world see your heavenly Father's love shine through you. As I mentioned before, your love with ABBA and how he loves you is what causes you to want to share his love with others.

1 John 3:16 is a perfect example of how much the Father loves us. He sent his only begotten son for us.

Jesus commanded his followers/disciples to spread His teachings to all the nations of the world. The whole purpose for Christ to come was for his lost creation to be returned into "right" relationship with the Father. He desires for the lost to be saved. Luke 19:10 (NIV)says "For the son of man is come to seek and to save that which is lost." Witnessing to the loss is not standing on the corner screaming, "The kingdom of heaven is at hand." It is telling someone of the love of Jesus in the grocery, at the park or even in the parking lot of the gym. The key is to live a life that displays God's agape love, to be sensitive to the Holy Spirit when he is moving you to share the gospel of Christ. And lastly, be committed to spreading the gospel, be excited about sharing the good news about how God saved your life. Share your experiences, and how he has brought you through your trials.

Reference scriptures:

Matt. 4:19, Matt. 9:37-38, Acts 1:8
Luke 15:10, Luke 24:46-47, John 20:21

A LETTER FROM GOD

Dear children,
I'm writing this letter to remind you that I am God,
but I am hurting.
You see, it hurts me to see my people in such a terrible state,
and all because you don't believe.
You don't believe that (I) God can do the impossible, after
all, I am the one who made the sun, the moon, the stars, the
earth and all that is in it. I even created you.
And even after doing all this I can still bless you
abundantly above all that you can ask or think, I can still
move mountains,
I can still heal the sick and raise the dead.
I can fill you with unspeakable joy.
I can fill your heart with unconditional love,
I can deliver you from every addiction and affliction,
I can feed you when you're hungry, give you a drink,
When you're thirsty, open doors that man cannot shut.
And close doors that man can't open,
You see, I can say, "yes," when man says, "no!"
And when the doctors say you're going to die, I can say live.
When you think now this is impossible for me to handle, I
can say give it to me. You may wonder, how is he able to
do all these things? Well, it's simple, because I am God!
And God alone.

'Nevertheless, I will bring health and healing to it; I will heal
my people and will let them enjoy abundant
peace and security.
Jeremiah 33:6

Fear not, for I am with you; Be not
dismayed, for I am your God. I will
strengthen you, Yes, I will help you, I
will uphold you with My righteous
right hand.'
Isaiah 41:10

Who his own self bare our sins in his own body on the tree,
that we, being dead to sins, should live unto righteousness:
by whose stripes ye were healed.
1 Peter 2:24

God requires us to have faith in him. According to Hebrews
11:6 KJV, But without faith [it is] impossible to please [him]:
for he that cometh to God must believe that he is, and [that]
he is a rewarder of them that diligently seek him. We cannot
please him if we do not have faith in his word and what he
promised us. Let us live a life of Faith, Hope, and Love. Have
faith in what his word says. We should entrust him with our
husbands, children, and our grandchildren. We are to trust
him with every aspect of what concerns us.

Reference Scriptures:
Isaiah 45:5, Isaiah 44:6, Ephesians 4:4-6,
1 Corinthians 8:6

REMOVE THE BANDAGES

All the years that have gone by, and it still hurts as if it
were yesterday. I am now practically covered with
bandages. I take a look at myself and finally realize that I
have become like a mummy (the walking dead) it is time,
it's time! Oh, so many years of trying to cover my pain. But
no more. Lord I cry unto thee!
Heal my broken heart.
Remove the bandages!
The time has come to remove the bandages.
Set me free Lord.
I want to live and not die.
I want to live a lively life.
I stand with my arms open wide,
waiting for your healing hands to overtake me.
And as you gently began to remove the bandages.
I slowly begin to fall back into your loving arms
to receive my complete healing. Now feeling ever
so free and joyful for the first time.
I am able to see my reflection in the mirror, revealing my
true identity, that strong, bold, woman of God, I have
always been.

And now as I look up to heaven with My
arms stretched wide.
I praise you with my new found liberty.
Thank you, Lord, for loving my broken heart back to pieces.

He healeth the broken in heart, and bindeth up their
wounds.
Psalms 147:3 KJV

Fear thou not; for I [am] with thee: be not dismayed; for I
[am] thy God: I will strengthen thee; yea, I will help thee;
yea, I will uphold thee with the right hand of my
righteousness.
Isaiah 41:10 KJV

Many times, women are the primary caregivers of their households, and in some cases to extended family members. Women naturally nurture, and provide emotional support to their families, friends and oftentimes co-workers. I found myself in this position at a very young age. The weight of knowing so many people depended on me and looked up to me was heavy. I began just putting band aids on my hurts to help others. We must realize that not only is God our source for everything, but he is the source for ALL. We must understand that in order to care and love others we must first care for and love ourselves. Know that you are valuable and important. You are the apple of ABBA's eye. Philippians 1:6 KJV, Being confident of this very thing, that he which hath begun a good work in you will perform it until the day of Jesus Christ. Don't try to care for your loved ones out of your own strength. We must trust that God loves our husbands, children and loved ones just as much as he loves us. Trust the process in their lives and allow him to do his healing work in your life, and theirs.

Allow him to complete the good work he started in their lives.

Reference Scriptures:
Matthew 11:28-30, John 16:33

TRUE LOVE

Dear Lord,
I just wanted to write you this letter to let you know how
much I love you. You see, I have finally learned that you are
my one and only true love, For years I have looked for
unconditional love in people
and each time I was failed.
But you Lord have never failed me yet.
You have always been there for me.
No matter what time of the day or night.
No matter the circumstance you have been there.
Whenever I feel down, you lift me up.
Whenever I have felt sad you give me joy.
And those times I was sick you healed my body.
It was you who fed me when I was hungry.
And when I felt lonely you came to comfort me.
Your love is an unfailing love,
it's an everlasting love,
it's patient and it's kind,
It's unconditional love.
Your love, Lord, has taught me how to love my enemies,
It has taught me how to see others as you see them.
For the love you have shown me,
I can now show others.
But there is one thing that I am unsure of,
and that is why you love me so?

11

That I may never come to know.
But still I take comfort in knowing that you loved me
enough to give your very life for me. You gave your very life
that I might be free,
That I might have an everlasting life.
You looked beyond all my faults and saw my needs.
And that I shall never forget!
I shall never forget my first,
My one and only true love.

1 John 4:18 KJV There is no fear in love; but perfect love
casteth out fear: because fear hath torment. He that feareth is
not made perfect in love.

Romans 5:8 KJV But God commendeth his love toward us, in
that, while we were yet sinners, Christ died for us.

John 3:16 KJV For God so loved the world, that he gave his
only begotten Son, that whosoever believeth in him should
not perish, but have everlasting life.

John 3:16 shows us a great example of the Father's unconditional love for his creation. He loved us enough to send his son Jesus to carry our burdens and die for our sins. I grew up without my father in the picture. It left me feeling abandoned. I felt like there was something missing. I spent many years trying to fill that void. I looked in all the wrong places, I looked for love from men, from toxic friendships, substance abuse, and alcohol. It wasn't until I developed a personal relationship with Jesus, that I realized that he was what I needed in my life. He is the only one that could fill the void in my heart. Oftentimes we are searching for something and just can't seem to find it. The missing piece to the puzzle is ABBA, father. No matter where you are in your walk, or in life. Look to God, he is the answer to all things.

Reference Scriptures:
1 John 4:4-11, 1John 4:16, 1 Peter 4:8, 1 Corinthians 13:1-13

THE PEACE OF GOD

And the peace of God shall rule in my heart.
No matter what I'm going through I have the right to go
through it with the peace of God ruling in my heart. Because
I know without doubt my father
will bring me through.
For my God is faithful.
He is faithful.
No matter what it looks like in the natural, he is faithful.
No matter what man says, God is faithful,
for his word says in Numbers 23:19, "God is not a man, that
He should lie, Nor a son of man, that He should repent. Has
He said, and will He not do it? Or has He spoken and will
not make it good and fulfill it?"
So, whatever his word says concerning my life and
any circumstance that comes my way his word will not come
back void but it will accomplish what it was set out to do.
For his word is true.
For his word IS the truth.
It's the truth.
His word is the reality in our lives.
For what we see in the natural is only what the enemy wants
us to believe. But what is seen in the spirit is the true reality.
Therefore, do not deny your spirit man his
spiritual food for he will then in return starve to death.

14

But on the other hand if you feed your spirit
man his rightful food
which is the word of God, he will then grow and mature in
many ways. He will grow to become stronger than the flesh.
For our wrestle is not against flesh and blood, but against
principalities, against the rulers of darkness.
Which is in the spirit realm,
then we will be prepared to fight the battle
and win because we have clothed ourselves in the
full armor of God.
I tell you this that you may be strengthened in your spirits &
not in flesh, that we may all live as righteous
women of God, holy and acceptable unto him who is able to
keep us from falling, that we may share in his glory forever
and ever amen.

As trials and life's troubles come our way, it is easy to lose
focus of Jesus and what he has done for us on the cross. After
surrendering our life over to Christ, and into our hearts. We
become joint heirs, (sons & daughters). The enemy would have
us focus on the trial at hand. He wants us to get consumed with
stress and worry, doubting what the word says about our lives.
We must not lose sight of whose we are and who we are.
According to Colossians 2:12, Our identity is hidden in Jesus
Christ. This means that it is no longer you, but Christ who lives
inside of you. You take on his attributes and his identity, you
can find this in Galatians 2:20. It is his life that now flows
through you. The old you was buried when he died on the
cross. And the new you rose with Christ. Take back your peace,
take back your joy, take back your confidence in God's word. It
is your right as a joint heir to the throne.

15

Colossians 3:1-2 KJV, "If ye then be risen with Christ, seek those things which are above, where Christ sitteth on the right hand of God. Set your affection on things above, not on things on the earth."

Reference Scriptures:

Matthew 24:35, Psalm 34:5-7, Hebrew 11:6, Colossians 3:15-17

A WOMAN OF NOBLE CHARACTER

A woman of noble character who can find? Lord I want so much to be that noble woman of character, But am I strong enough and will I be able to stand? Will I still be able to bless your name during my storms or will I be weak when my husband needs to be encouraged and my children are crying out for help? Will I be able to speak life to the man you have blessed me with,

oh there is no doubt in my mind, yes, I love him! But oh!! My God, so much pain he has caused me! So many dark days and so many sleepless nights and yet still I remember the promises that (you) have made,

how you would bless me and my family.

The work you said we would do.

How you called us to your ministry as one to
be on one accord.

So, because I have faith in you!

Because I trust in you, because I know that you are faithful to complete in us what you said you would, yes, I shall stand!

I shall be strong for I am that noble woman of character!
For I shall speak life to my husband! I shall encourage him!
And yes, I can answer my children's cries for help.

17

For I shall stand, I shall stand!
I!! Shall!! Stand!!

Proverbs 31:10 gives us an example of a noble woman, a virtuous woman. The Amplified version says, "An excellent woman [one who is spiritual, capable, intelligent, and virtuous]." The word noble means: having, showing, or coming from personal qualities that people admire (such as honesty, generosity, courage, etc.). As women of God, mothers, and wives we must stand on the word of God for our families, churches, communities, and for our country. God wants us to have confidence in his word despite what we see. To live a life of holiness, to not just put on the garment of unconditional love but for it to be a part of who we are. He desires that we live a life that embodies who he is, which is love. We are to dress in strength and dignity, while standing strong on God's unchanging word. His word is what will guide us during times of uncertainty, or times of struggle. Psalms 119:105 KJV, Thy word is a lamp unto my feet, and a light unto my path. Hebrews 11:1 KJV, Now faith is the substance of things hoped for, the evidence of things not seen. Take some time today as you meditate on scripture and ask God if you are reflecting his love, if you are displaying the attributes of a noble woman of character.

Reference Scriptures:
1 John 4:7-21, Proverbs 3:5-6, Luke 1:37, Hebrews 11:1, 1 Corinthians 13:1-13

BATTLEFIELDS OF THE MIND

Sometimes even after we have given our lives to Christ,
somehow, we let Satan hold us captive.
We become his prisoner, a slave to his devices.
Not knowing who we are in the Lord,
the enemy holds our minds captive, unable to
let our loved ones,
our pastors, our friends know that there is a battle going on
in our minds. Prisoners come in all shapes and sizes.
A loving mother and devoted wife, strong on the outside,
but dying on the inside wanting to end her life.
Held captive in her past, still dealing with those things that
she was so much ashamed of. If she only knew that when
she gave her life to Christ,
asked him to forgive her of her sins, and
let him into her heart,
He threw her sins into the sea of forgetfulness, never to be
remembered. If she only knew that she is now a new
creation in Christ,
A New Creation.
So as the wicked one tries to hold us prisoner.
Telling us that someone will find out our horrible past or
when he tries to torment us by playing over and over again
in our minds the wrong streets we've all turned down once
in our lives, we can now let him know,

19

it does not have to be a secret,
but it's a testimony of where God and his precious mercy
and saving grace has brought us from.
So, you see what we have gone through
or been brought out of might be what a fellow sister is going
through right now and our very testimony might just be the
one thing she needed
to let her know that God can also save her life.
So, our minds must stay renewed with the word of God and
we must never be ashamed of how good God has been to us
and where he has brought us from.

Romans 12:2 NIV tells us, "Do not conform to the pattern of this world, but be transformed by the renewing of your mind. Then you will be able to test and approve what God's will is, his good, pleasing and perfect will." Staying in the word and keeping our mind on the things of God is key.

Philippians 4:8 ESV, "Finally, brethren, whatsoever things are true, whatsoever things are honest, whatsoever things are just, whatsoever things are pure, whatsoever things are lovely, whatsoever things are of good report; if there be any virtue, and if there be any praise, think on these things."

Reference scriptures:
Proverbs 23:7, 2 Corinthians 10:5, 2 Timothy 1:7

THE APOSTLE AND THE DOCTOR

The Apostle stands strong and tall.
He walks with his head held high.
Signs of war wounds are nowhere to be found.
And as he cases the area for danger, he motions for the
Doctor to join him. And as she stands by his side, she looks
at him and says,
"The mountain was steep, and the climb was hard,
but we made it."
Then, he nods his head and agrees without
even saying a word.
They both sigh.
Now standing back-to-back, heart to heart, with a sword in
his hand, a sword in hers, they are both dressed for battle
and ready to fight. Now he is very noble and kind. He
stands tall like a giant, but he is gentle like a dove. Now
the Doctor!

Well, she is bold,
confident and strong in the Lord. And when he's on the
battlefield his roar is like a lion. And her strength is like
that of a lioness defending her cub. He fights long and
hard for his territory, and finally, the enemy gives way.

He looks and notices blood dripping from his hands. He frantically checks himself only to find that not even a hair on his head was touched. Now throughout the battle not once was there mention of the Doctor, Where has she been?
Would she leave the Apostle alone in the battle?
No, for even in battle they stand back-to-back, heart to heart.
You see, when he strikes, she guards,
when she strikes, he guards.
They fight hand in hand.
And as they walk away from the battlefield,
they walk hand in hand with their swords held up to the sky singing victory, victory shall be mine!

Ephesians 6:10 Teaches us that we must be strong in the Lord and in the power of his might. We must never take off our battle clothes which are the armor of God. Colossians 3:14 NIV,

"And over all these virtues put on love, which binds them all together in perfect unity." Often in marriage, we miss the importance of fighting on the battlefield together. We can sometimes get caught up in the everyday hustle and doing ministry that we forget to have intimacy together with the Father. We should pray together and study the word together. We are stronger together. May Yahweh make your marriage strong and may you and your spouse both be like a tree planted by streams of water, that meditate on him day and night keeping his statues in your hearts.

Reference scriptures:
Ecclesiastes 4:9-12, Joshua 1:9, Psalm 1:1-3

AND... THROUGH THE STORM

When you look into my eyes what do you see?
Does the bright smile cover the pain?
If I still come to church and act as if nothing is wrong
maybe no one will know, how much I am hurting. For
indeed I'm hurting.
But if I take slow deep breaths and not make too much eye
contact, then no one will know. Because I must stay strong,
so many see me as such a strong woman of God. I can't let
them know that my pain has become so unbearable that I
could hardly breath,
and here I am chatting with a fellow sister in Christ, telling
her that everything will be alright. And that if she holds on,
God will make a way. My eyes are now beginning to tear,
but before anyone sees (excuse me I'll talk to you later) and
as I rush off to the ladies' room to hide the great pain that I
am suffering, the tears begin to fall.
And as I close the door to finally release,
I wonder if God will bring me through?
Has he forgotten me?
Does he still love me?
"What have I done wrong?" I ask!!

And as my mind begins to race with so many questions and
doubts. I remember that my heavenly Father,
He left me a living will of all the things that belong to him,
that now belong to me.
So, I take a deep breath, close my eyes and raise my hands
and say, "Lord!!!! I trust in you."
I trust your word, which is the living will you prepared for
me, because you knew that this day and hour would come.
So, as I study your word, I am strengthened to handle
everything that comes my way. So, now Lord, I thank you
for loving me, just as I am.

There was a time in my faith walk, where I thought that I
needed to always show strength. As a leader in the Church, I
thought that because so many people looked up to me that I
could not show weakness or pain. I learned that this is just
another trick of the enemy. In fact, as a leader, showing that
you go through the same things that the people who look up
to you do, can teach them how to persevere and press. It keeps
you from falling into the trap of religion. While others are
looking up to you, they can see God completing his perfect
work through you as you continue to grow. Be transparent,
and truthful, this will be more of a witness to those entrusted
to you than you pretending that everything is always going
good. 1 Peter 5:8-10 KJV, "Be sober, be vigilant; because your
adversary the devil, as a roaring lion, walketh about, seeking
whom he may devour: Whom resist steadfast in the faith,
knowing that the same afflictions are accomplished in your
brethren that are in the world. But the God of all grace, who
hath called us unto his eternal glory by Christ Jesus, after that
ye have suffered a while, make you perfect, establish,
strengthen, settle you."

24

Reference Scriptures:
1 Corinthians 15:58, Philippians 1:27, 2 Timothy 2:15

THE JOY OF THE LORD IS MY STRENGTH

When it seems as though I'm all alone,
The joy of the Lord is my strength.
Even though I've been hurt so many times,
The joy of the Lord is still my strength.
During testing and trials
The joy of the Lord is my strength.
The joy of the Lord is my strength.
It is my strength, because of his love
I am able to look in the face of those who have tried to
slander my name, and smile,
with the peace that surpasses all understanding in my heart.
His joy is my Strength!
My strength is in his joy!

No matter the storm or trial, ABBA wants us to know that our strength can be found in the joy he freely gave to us. We just have to rest in it. It should be a place of rest for us. James 1:2-3 NIV says, "consider it pure joy, my brothers and sisters, whenever you face trials of many kinds, because you know that the testing of your faith produces perseverance." How we respond to life and its circumstances matter. Will you trust him no matter what it looks like, or will you let the trials of life weigh you down? Romans 15:13 NIV says, "May the God of hope fill you with all joy and peace as you trust in him, so that you may overflow with hope by the power of the Holy Spirit."

Reference scriptures:
Philippians 4:4-7, Proverbs 17:22

A FATHER'S LOVE

I am your father and I love you.
I love you more than you can ever imagine,
so much that I sent down my only Son to die for you,
to die that you might have life, life abundantly.
Just take a moment and think about that.
Your only child!
I sacrificed innocent blood for you.
Oh, my children, hear me when I say that my love for
you is immeasurable.
I love you enough to move mountains,
enough to rain down bread from heaven,
I even love you enough to part the greatest sea, just
so you can cross to the other side and escape the
hand of your enemy. I love you enough to correct
you when you're wrong,
and commend you when you're right. I love you enough to
feed you when you're hungry and give you a
drink when you're thirsty.
Enough to go down into the pit and snatch the
keys of life and death from the Fowler and take
back every right and authority you now have. I
love you enough to cast your sins into the dept of
the sea when you come to me with a heart of
repentance.
what I want you to understand is that **love** it's the key,
as I have loved you, so I have commanded you to love.

So, my children, do what is right and pleasing in my sight, "love," you are to love your neighbors, love your brothers and sisters, love your enemies, love when it feels good and love when it hurts, I want you to love one another, Love one another.

I command that you love one another as I have loved you. For I have loved you when you didn't love me back.

I have loved you when you were strong, and I have loved you in your weakness,

I have loved you when you were right, and I have loved you when you were wrong. I have loved you through your darkest hour so that you may see the light. So, you must love your fellow brother when he's right or when he's wrong.

You must love whether he's up or whether he is down. Because if it had not been for my love for you, where would you be?

John 15:12 NIV tells us, "My commandment is this, love each other as I have loved you." God expects his children to love others with the same unconditional love he shares with us.

The way we love others is what separates us from the world. This is how the world recognizes

that we are followers of the Messiah. Whoever does not love does not know God, for God **is love.** 1 Corinthians 13:13 NIV says, "And now these three remain: faith, hope and love. But the greatest of these is love." His love never fails, so if we are his children we will love with that same love, never losing hope and always abounding in love for humanity.

Reference scriptures:
1 John 4:7-21, John 3:16, Isaiah 54:10

Tonia L. Riley

A MOTHERS LOVE

A mother, she is first blessed in giving birth.
She is courageous and daring,
She can also be violent when her child is in
danger of being attacked.
She corrects, she disciplines, she reaches out with an
unconditional love, she gives, and she gives, even though
sometimes she doesn't get back. She pours out everything
she has inside her to her children,
she boasts on her children's accomplishments and cheers
them on in their failures. Who is this that I speak of…?
She's a mother.
You know, the woman down the street who
opens her home to the less fortunate child.
Or what about the lady who gets up every morning at 5 a.m.
To make sure her child doesn't go unfed. You know, the
one you pass by every day sitting at the bus stop.
Or what about the one who's first at the office
and the last to leave.

What I want you to understand is, no
matter what shape, size, color, or form
your mother is, you should honor her
as the Word says,
So, remember when you're driving, or
at work or maybe even sitting at a bus
stop and you see a mother nearby.

Remember your mother and how precious she is
and know that God knows our needs before we need them,
so therefore, honor your mother in all her beauty, and all
her ways in all her ups and in all her downs,
God gave you to her because she was just what you needed.

As a child I would look at my friend's mothers and wish that I had a mother like theirs. As I became an adult and matured in the spirit, I realized that my mother carried everything I needed in her. Even in her struggles, I learned that those times of heartache and pain is what helped to mold me into the strong woman I am today. I did not just learn the lessons my mother taught me, but I learned from the things she did not teach me, the things I saw by watching her go through life. My mother gave me all she had to give. While allowing God's loving touch to heal me in those broken places, I was reminded of 1 Peter 4:8 NIV, "Above all, keep loving one another earnestly, since love covers a multitude of sins." I was no longer angry for what my mother couldn't do but was thankful for what she did give. This is where my healing came into full manifestation. So, if you have experienced hurt during your childhood, choose to love and forgive. Let God bring healing to those broken areas. I realized that I could still honor my parents, even when I didn't agree with everything they did, said or didn't do.

Reference Scriptures:
Exodus 20:12, Proverbs 1:8-9, Ephesians 6:1-3

LEFT ALONE

Now after everyone has gone home & there are
no more tears left to cry. The cards have stopped
coming, the phone has now stopped ringing.
No more sending flowers to help brighten
up my darkened days.
Wall to wall people had filled the house, oh how I miss you,
that is no doubt, and all of a sudden, I turn to see that there
is no one else left standing here but me. That's when I begin
to feel the deepest depth of my saddened pain.
As I search past my pain, and now I can finally see that
Lord your love has always been there for me. In so many
ways, many have touched my heart
in this time of need.
But after it's all said and done, it's your love
Lord that can ease my pain. Left alone! No!
You see, your love surrounds me wherever I go and
whatever I'm doing. As I take a walk in the lovely
summer weather, I feel a soft touch across my
cheek. While I stare out the window, your peace
comes to rest upon my shoulders. And as I sit at
the table to drink a cup of coffee a thought of my
dear husband crosses my mind, and at that very
instant I feel God's everlasting love overwhelm
me. So, Ma, never feel left alone

because God's comforting love is unchanging,
unconditional,
everlasting and most of all his love,
is more powerful than any situation that comes our way. So,
know that as he loves your broken heart back to pieces.
Understand that as you go through your healing process,
that God is all seeing, all knowing, all powerful, all loving,
all understanding. And he loves you enough to never leave
you alone.

Dealing with the death of a loved one is not an easy task, but with God's help we can overcome the feeling of loneliness and grief. Joshua 1:5 ESV, "No man shall be able to stand before you all the days of your life. Just as I was with Moses, so shall I be with you. I will not leave you or forsake you." Let the word of God comfort you in your time of need. Allow him to speak to your heart, give him everything that concerns you. He gives us a time to mourn but be careful not to stay there. Ecclesiastes 3:1 KJV says, "To every thing there is a season, and time to every purpose under heaven:." Let the Fathers love, and peace be our portion during the loss of loved ones. Let him walk you through this difficult season in your life.

Reference Scriptures:
Ecclesiastes 3: 2-8, John 14:27, numbers 6:26

JOY

Yes, she left,
so soft and so swift,
anticipating getting her wings back.
Soft and so swift,
God bought her home.
To dance with angels
and as she sweeps back and forth around the throne room,
laughing and singing.
She pauses for just a moment, to say, don't cry, don't cry
daddy, don't cry mommy.
I'm okay, for with Jesus I play and in God's arms I rest.
In the Father's arms that's where I'll be.
Cuddled so tight resting so sound.
In the Father's arms, that's where you'll find me
Waiting till that special day, the day we'll meet again.
But for now, in the Father's arms that's where I'll be.

Losing a child at any stage in life is very difficult. No matter if you have lost a child through a miscarriage, or a tubal pregnancy. Whether it was during childbirth or a few months after they were born, at the age of 7 or even at the age of 18. You still feel pain, no matter the age, it doesn't hurt any less. You still experience the pain of losing a child. You feel that brokenness of heart. There are no amount of words that can take the pain away. The answer to this hurt is the love, and comfort of the Father. Isaiah 41:10 ESV says "Fear not for I am with you: be not dismayed, for I am your God: I will strengthen you, I will help you, I will uphold you with my righteous right hand. He will be with you every step of the way; he will uphold you.

Reference Scriptures:
Matthew 5:4, Psalms 34:18, Revelation 21:4

ONE

And as I lay here awake in bed, I can feel the comfort of our
two bodies coming together, becoming a sculptured image
of God's very word,
(AND NOW THE TWO HAVE BECOME ONE) not only in
the natural but in spirit. As I press my back against his
chest, I begin feeling his very heartbeat,
now my heart begins to study the rhythm of his heart, our
two hearts are now beating together making a song of love,
faith, strength, and courage.
His hand in mine and mine in his.
His strong body form begins to strengthen who I am in God.
And in return my soft touch embraces the
longing of his soul,
while caressing that untouched place in which I carry the
only key.
Now so full of my love, he grants my
deepest desires, his love running so deep
within my heart overflows, spilling into
every corner of my soul.
And as our love collides, we sing praise to our God from the
inside out filling the air with a sweet fragrance
ever so pleasing
in the nostrils of our Lord and Savior.

Genesis 2:24 ESV tells us, "Therefore a man shall leave his father and mother and hold fast to his wife, and they shall become one flesh." When man and woman come together as husband and wife, they become one. Marriage is a sacred covenant between man, woman, and God. You are not only coming into covenant with your husband or wife, but you are also coming into covenant with Yahweh. So, make sure that you take it seriously. The proper order of things is God, family (which is husband & children), then the church. This does not mean to neglect your calling, but simply that you must make sure that the home-front is your first ministry. Put the time in to build a strong foundation with your husband, so as you both go out into ministry, home is always safe and secure. Take time to build relationship with one another, communication is key when laying each brick. Have fun and take pleasure in one another. Enjoy your differences and laugh often. Most importantly God should be the foundation of your union.

Reference Scriptures:
Proverbs 5:18, Ephesians 4:2-3, Colossians 3:14, Ephesians 5:25-33, 1 Corinthians 13:2, Ecclesiastes 4:12

WALKING WITH YOU

Let me walk beside you in the sunlight and the rain,
let me share your joys,
triumphs and your times of pain.
Let me be your lover, partner, best friend, and confidant,
for you are all I'll ever need and all I'll ever want.
You're my special friend
my dearest dream come true...
no one will ever love someone as much as I love you.

Ephesians 5:21 NIV tell us that husbands and wives should submit one to another. Marriage is a partnership. God and his word are the glue that will hold your marriage together. You will have good times and bad times, just hold on to what God has promised. 1 Peter 4:8, "Above all, love each other deeply, because love covers a multitude of sins." Continue to see your spouse as the same man you feel deeply in love with, even when he may be struggling or at his worst. Love him through those times and continue to speak the word over his life and be his friend.

Reference Scriptures:
John 15:12, Colossians 3:14, Proverbs 17:17

A TRIBUTE TO MY GRANDMOTHER

Grandmother
Thank you for the joy you bring.
Thank you for the love you sing.
I enjoyed the times spent sitting at your feet
as you poured wisdom upon my head. How
you make everyone whose life you pass feel
that they have meaning. I remember sitting
and watching as you poured yourself into
every meal. Though time has passed by your
precious face, and your beautiful soft hair has
now turned gray.
Just know that to me, still every word you speak leaves an
example of wisdom. I never thought a single person could
give so much to so many others. In every way with each
passing day the thought of my grandmother and how
precious and dear, and gentle, and loving and giving of
herself she is passes my mind.
You've touched my heart in ways I could never explain. It
still amazes me how you make everyone who loves you
feel like they're your special love.
Grandma I love you.
I love you for your beauty,
I love you for the wisdom you give,
the joy you spread and the love you share.

My love for you just keeps growing & growing.
Grandma, I know this walk for you has been long and hard.
But yet, it's been rewarding and joyful, surprising,
Comforting but most of all blessed.
For all the wisdom, joy, love, kindness
and teaching you have given not only to me but to so many
others will last for a lifetime. My heart overflows
with love for you.
Thank you for giving so much to me.
Thank you so much for being so strong for so many others.
Thank you for all the mornings I was awakened
to your joyous voice ringing through the house as you sang
praises to God and the smell of coffee filling the air.
Thank you for all the prayers, the tears, the joy,
the love and all the strengthen, peace, comfort, wisdom,
patience and all the examples, the direction, all the sweat, all
the cooking, the reassuring and all the talks.
Thank you for the wiping of tears.
Thank you for standing when no one else was willing
and thank you for interceding.
Because it paid off.
Mommy just know, that in me, in my life it paid off.
Because of who you are, I have a chance, you have given me
a chance. Thank you for pouring so much into
my life in so many ways.
You have helped mold me into the strong, bold, & virtuous
woman that I am today. So now open your heart and receive
that same love you have poured into my life. Grandma I love
you and thank you so much.
Loving you always,
your granddaughter, Tonia

If you have enjoyed this book, Tonia would love to hear about it.

Kindly leave her a review on Amazon.

71973487R00028